Radford Public Library
30 W. Main St.
Radford, VA 24141

DISCARD

S0-BSD-776

UNIVERSITY OF
Dublin
TRINITY COLLEGE

Jungle School

Elizabeth Laird • Roz Davison • David Sim

APR 1 6 2007

Crabtree Publishing Company
www.crabtreebooks.com

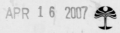

PMB 16A, 350 Fifth Avenue,
Suite 3308,
New York, NY 10118

616 Welland Avenue,
St. Catharines, Ontario
Canada, L2M 5V6

Laird, Elizabeth.
  Jungle School / written by Elizabeth Laird and Roz Davison;
illustrated by David Sim.
    p. cm. -- (Green bananas)
  Summary: New at school, Jani shows her monkey classmates all the ways that
her wheelchair makes her special.
  ISBN-13: 978-0-7787-1026-4 (rlb) -- ISBN-10: 0-7787-1026-2 (rlb)
  ISBN-13: 978-0-7787-1042-4 (pbk) -- ISBN-10: 0-7787-1042-4 (pbk)
  [1. People with disabilities--Fiction. 2. Wheelchairs--Fiction. 3.
Monkeys--Fiction. 4. Schools--Fiction.] I. Davison, Roz. II. Sim, David,
ill. III. Title. IV. Series.

  PZ7.L1579Jun 2006
  [E]--dc22

                                          2005034959

                                             LC

Published by Crabtree Publishing in 2006
First published in 2006 by Egmont Books Ltd.
Text copyright © Elizabeth Laird and Roz Davison 2006
Illustrations copyright © David Sim 2006
The Author and Illustrator have asserted their moral rights.
Paperback ISBN 0-7787-1042-4
Reinforced Hardcover Binding ISBN 0-7787-1026-2

1 2 3 4 5 6 7 8 9 0 Printed in Italy 5 4 3 2 1 0 9 8 7 6
All rights reserved. No part of this publication may be reproduced, stored in a retrieval system or
be transmitted in any form or by any means, electronic, mechanical, photocopying, recording, or
otherwise, without the prior written permission of Crabtree Publishing Company.

FIRST DAY
AT SCHOOL

WELL DONE,
JANI!

YOU CHEEKY
MONKEY!

Green Bananas

For Amy, Olivia, and Phoebe Jones
R. D.

For Rachel
D. S.

FIRST DAY AT SCHOOL

It was Jani's first day at Jungle
School.

All the little monkeys stared at her.

She didn't like being the new girl.

"Come on, Jani," said Miss Mango.

"Don't be shy."

One monkey waved at Jani.

"Hi," he said. "I'm Abe."

Hello, Jani.

Another monkey smiled at her.

"Hello," she said. "I'm Olivia."

Jani went to sit at their table.

"Why does your chair have wheels?"

asked Abe.

"Because my legs aren't very strong,"

said Jani.

"How do you make it move?"

asked Olivia.

"With my hands," said Jani.

"Like this."

All the other monkeys just stared.

"Do you mind people staring at you?" asked Olivia.

"New girls always get stared at," said Jani. "Sometimes it's OK and I feel like a movie star."

"But sometimes it's rude, and I don't like it at all."

"Playtime!" said Miss Mango.

The little monkeys all began to skip
and run around.

"I'll hold the skipping rope," said Jani.

"I'll hold the other end,"

said Olivia.

I'm tired.

The skipping rope went around and around and around.

Me Tarzan!

Jani wasn't tired. Her arms were very strong.

Abe ran up to her.

"Can I have a ride on your

wheelchair?" he asked.

"OK," said Jani.

"Can I?" asked Olivia.

"Yes!" said Jani.

The other monkeys stared and

jumped up and down. They shouted,

"Me too! Me too!"

"I like Jungle School," said Jani.

"I don't feel like the new girl any more."

WELL DONE, JANI!

Later it was gym class.

"Today we're going to pick things up with our tails," said Miss Mango. "Watch me, everyone."

21

The monkeys stood in a line.

It was difficult for Jani to reach the

hoop with her tail.

22

Then she had an idea.

"Can I do my own exercise?"

she asked.

"Sure, Jani," said Miss Mango.

Jani raced her chair up and down.

She went around and around in circles.

All the other monkeys stopped what

they were doing and watched her.

Jani didn't stop until she was

tired out.

"I really like your chair," said Olivia.

"So do I," said Jani. "It's what makes

me me."

"What do you mean?" asked Olivia and Abe.

"Well, we are all different, aren't we?" said Jani.

"Some of us are short, and some of us are tall."

29

"Some of us are good at swatting

flies. And some of us aren't."

"And some people have chairs with wheels. Like you!" said Abe.

"Come on, monkeys!" said Miss

Mango. "Catch!" And she threw

some balls up high.

Abe caught a green one.

Olivia caught a pink one.

But Jani caught a yellow one AND

a blue one.

"Well done, Jani," said Miss Mango.

And all the other monkeys clapped.

Miss Mango got out the

dress-up box.

Jani was very happy.

She liked dressing up.

The other monkeys all ran to the
box. They began to pull things out.

"I could be a princess," she thought.

"Or a cowgirl. Or what about a

pirate!"

"Stand back, all of you," said
Miss Mango. "Now, what do you
want, Abe?"

"The wizard's cloak," said Abe.
"I want to be a rabbit," said Olivia.

"And what do you want, Jani?" said

Miss Mango.

"May I please have the pirate hat?"

asked Jani.

Jani looked great in the pirate hat.

"Which ribbon should my parrot

wear?" she asked.

"Black's cool," said Abe. "Like my cloak."

"Pink's pretty," said Olivia.

"Oh no," said Jani. "I like yellow."

Everyone was dressed up now.

They all began to play.

Abe tried to put a spell on Jani.

He wanted to turn her into a frog.

Olivia pretended to be Jani's pet

rabbit. Jani stroked her ears.

Miss Mango took out her camera.

"Well done, monkeys," she said.

"Smile, please, everyone!"

But what is Jani up to?

Oh! She's dressed up just like

Miss Mango!

"You cheeky monkey!" said

Miss Mango, laughing.